This is Farmer Fred. He is a busy
farmer with lots of animals to
look after.

A catalogue record for this book is available from the British Library

Published by Ladybird Books Ltd
80 Strand London WC2R 0RL
A Penguin Company

13 15 17 19 20 18 16 14 12

Illustrations © Emma Dodd MMII

LADYBIRD and the device of a Ladybird are trademarks of Ladybird Books Ltd

Little Workmates

Farmer Fred

by Ronne Randall
illustrated by Emma Dodd

Ladybird

"Cock-a-doodle-doo!"
crowed the cockerel.
It was getting-up time
on the farm.

"Come on, Nell!"
said Farmer Fred.
"We've got lots to
do today!"

At breakfast, Mrs Farmer was upset.

"Peg the cat is missing," she said. "I think she's lost!"

"Don't worry," said Farmer Fred. "Nell and I will find her!"

In the farmyard, Farmer
Fred thought he heard a
"Meow!"

"Maybe Peg's in the
henhouse," he said to Nell.

In the henhouse, Della and Delilah were feeling very pleased. They had laid two eggs each!

"Cluck! cluck!" said Della.

"Cluck! cluck!" said Delilah. But where was Peg?

"Maybe Peg's in the pigsty?" said Farmer Fred. He put some feed in the trough for Primrose and her piglets.

"Oink!" said Primrose.

"Squeal, squeeeeal!" said her hungry little piglets.
But where was Peg?

"Perhaps Peg is in the barn?" said Farmer Fred.
He milked Daisy the cow while he was there.

"Moo!" said Daisy.
But where was Peg?

Suddenly Nell ran to
the hayloft.

"Woof! Woof! Woof!"
she barked.

"Hopping haystacks!"
said Farmer Fred,
"It's Peg!"

Farmer Fred found his ladder. But it was broken!

"I'll have to call Builder Bill!" he said.

Builder Bill arrived with his ladder. Farmer Fred climbed up to the hayloft.

"Woof! Woof!" barked Nell.

"Hopping haystacks!" said Farmer Fred. "You'll never guess what...!"

Peg had six fluffy little kittens!

"That's why she came up to the hayloft!" said Farmer Fred. "She wanted to have her babies where it was warm and quiet."

Mrs Farmer brought Peg a bowl of Daisy's fresh milk.

"Well done, Peg!" said Farmer Fred.

"Meow!" said Peg.

"Mew-mew!" said her six new kittens.

Soon it was time for tea.

"Hopping haystacks!" said Farmer Fred. "What an exciting day!"

"Woof! Woof!" agreed Nell.

This is Fireman Fergus. He is a brave firefighter and he has a good head for heights.

This is Nurse Nancy. She works hard looking after the patients at Story Town Hospital.

This is Builder Bill. He is a very good builder and his houses never fall down.

This is Queen Clara. She is a very good queen and all the people of Story Town love her.

This is Postman Pete. He loves delivering letters and parcels to everyone in Story Town.